The
CHAMPION
CHARLIES

Boot It

ADRIAN BECK

Illustrations by **Adele K. Thomas**

RANDOM HOUSE AUSTRALIA

A Random House book
Published by Penguin Random House Australia Pty Ltd
Level 3, 100 Pacific Highway, North Sydney NSW 2060
penguin.com.au

Penguin
Random House
Australia

First published by Random House Australia in 2018
Text copyright © Penguin Random House Australia 2018
Branding copyright © Football Federation Australia 2018
Illustration copyright © Adele K. Thomas 2018

Addresses for the Penguin Random House group of companies can be found at
global.penguinrandomhouse.com/offices.

A catalogue record for this
book is available from the
National Library of Australia

ISBN: 978 0 14379 126 3

Cover image and internal illustrations by Adele K. Thomas
Cover design by Tasha Dixon
Internal design and typesetting by Midland Typesetters, Australia
Printed in Australia by Griffin Press, an accredited ISO AS/NZS 14001:2004
Environmental Management System printer

Penguin Random House Australia uses papers that are natural, renewable
and recyclable products and made from wood grown in sustainable forests.
The logging and manufacturing processes are expected to conform to the
environmental regulations of the country of origin.

For all the kids who eat, sleep and breathe football!

CONTENTS

CHAPTER ONE

BLOWING IT IN THE WIND

Have you ever done your hair with a **LEAF—BLOWER?** Or ironed your shirt with the **EXHAUST** of a Boeing 747? Maybe you've tried to run directly into a **HURRICANE?**

Well, that's how CJ was feeling. It was so windy that his hair pointed straight out, like a cartoon character who'd just survived a TNT explosion. **BOOM!** You can try to control many aspects of a football game, but no-one can control the weather.

The Jindaberg Jets were deep into the second half of their game against the Dewberry Dugongs. The very **POSH** Dewberry Dugongs.

It was an 'away' match, on the edge of the Yarra River that was swirling in the blustery wind. The Dewberry Primary School's flagpoles almost seemed to be swaying and all the tree branches snaked around as if they were **ALIVE**. The parents in the crowd huddled beside the toilet blocks with the choppy water at their backs, shielding their faces with scarves, hats, expensive handbags and, in some cases, small yappy dogs. The wind even drowned out the Jets' karaoke coach, Mr Hyants (also known as **HIGHPANTS**), who was belting out advice in the form of song, even though no-one could hear a word of it – which wasn't such a bad thing.

But back to CJ . . .

He was shaken BIG TIME. Although not by the wind, and not even by the SWEATY TOUPEE, stolen by the gale that smacked him in the face at half-time. There was something else playing on his mind.

'Peekaboo, CJ!' cried Charlotte, as she whizzed past at such speed that her long ponytail was horizontal. 'Come on, fellow co-captain! Still 0–0. Can't be much left on the clock!'

'Peekaboo?' asked Benji, whose little legs pumped furiously as he sped past.

'Yep,' said CJ, breaking into a sprint. 'Peekaboo.'

'This is our last chance, dude,' said Benji. 'Forget that goal you missed in the first half!'

Thanks, Benji, thought CJ. *Aren't you meant to be my best mate? Not an ideal time to remind me I stuffed up a super simple shot.*

Lexi had the ball. She was lining up for a corner kick in the Jets' attack. She squinted into the wind. Her hair was even wilder than CJ's and – given she always liked to look her best – she was hating these conditions more than anyone. She'd even snapped at the Dewberry school photographer at half-time, 'No photos, PUH–LEASE!'

'Peekaboo!' yelled the Jets' keeper, the Paulveriser, from the top of his goal box. 'Move it, CJ! What's your problem?'

Sprinting to keep up, CJ's Dugong opponent narrowed his eyes. *Peekaboo* wasn't a term that was used all that often on a football pitch. It was certainly not a term that seemed natural coming from the Paulveriser either. (For the record, even *ooga booga* would've seemed too advanced for the Paulveriser). But *Peekaboo* was a Jets set play. Something Charlotte had them working on at practice. It was inspired by her baby sister, Sofia.

CJ thundered towards his position. If the set play was to work, CJ needed to get himself downfield to the top of the goal box. FAST.

Lexi covered her eyes. She did an actual peekaboo. This would've been a clever secret signal if almost every Jet hadn't already shouted out the term 'peekaboo' the moment Lexi had been awarded the corner.

Tingling all over, CJ arrived beside Saanvi, Charlotte and Benji at the top of the box.

'Nice of you to make it,' said Saanvi, sarcastically. The four of them jostled for position with the Dugong defenders. The eight players were all bunched up.

Charlotte glanced from Lexi to the defenders and back. She checked her angle on goal, then she prodded the grass, testing the surface. Charlotte was in the zone – she stared into the wind, weighing everything up. As CJ marvelled at Charlotte's focus, a drop of sweat trailed down his forehead. She probably noticed that too.

Lexi ran in for the kick.

'Now!' cried Charlotte.

PEEKABOO WAS ON!

The Jets scrambled into position. Benji bolted for the back post, making a nuisance of himself with defenders on the far side. (Nuisance? Perfect prankster-Benji mission). Saanvi stood tall where she was, right in the way of the nearest Dugongs. This allowed Charlotte and CJ to curve around the group at the top of the box and surge towards the nearest post.

In other words, CJ and Charlotte were popping out from the group of players to say PEEKABOO! to the ball.

Lexi placed the ball perfectly. Assisted by the wind, it was rocketing towards the area just in front of the near post.

Charlotte sidestepped closer to the centre of the goals. The Dugong goalie noticed. He arched back in her direction to stop her possible shot on goal. But CJ was right there, and with the goalie worried about Charlotte, there was now a gap for CJ to score. He leapt into the sky, and at full stretch he slammed his foot into the ball.

The back of the net wouldn't know what hit it!

Peeka-BOO—YEAH!

But the ball came off the side of CJ's foot.

7

It felt wrong IMMEDIATELY. The force of Lexi's kick meant the ball skewed upwards, high into the wind.

'No,' muttered CJ. 'No, no, no!'

CJ noticed Saanvi and Fahad's instant looks of disappointment.

The ball sailed on a gust, up into the sky, then towards the garden beside the Dewberry clubrooms. There was a gardener-type guy in overalls watering the flowers. And the ball was headed straight for him.

'Heads up!' warned CJ.

THONK!

Too late. The ball hit the gardener, smack on his noggin. He lost his balance and sprayed his hose. UP! Right over the top of the clubrooms. The water curved in the air and plummeted down onto the Dewberry parents huddled together on the other side.

'This won't end well,' said Charlotte.

The parents went wide-eyed as the water drenched the crowd. Everything happened all at once. Their mouths dropped. They tried to fling the water away. They stepped back, sideways, into each other. And a tall dad at the front squealed. To avoid the water, he backed into the group. With FORCE. The parents were all caught up in a bunch and they fell.

Almost all of them.

SPLOOSH!

Like lemmings.

SPLOOSH! SPLOOOOOSH!

Right off the rocky bank and into the freezing cold river.

SPLOOSH! SPLOOOOOSH! SPLOOOOOOOOSH!

'Oh, how awful,' said Lexi. 'So many expensive outfits ruined.'

FWWWWWEEEEEEEET!

The ref blew her whistle. GAME OVER.

CJ let out a long breath. He caught Charlotte's eye, then stared at the ground.

'Best unintentional prank ever, dude,' laughed Benji, slapping CJ on the back. 'They look like drowned rats. Classic!'

'Thanks,' said CJ, as the parents started helping each other out of the water.

The Jets and the Dugongs shook hands. The Jets were heading to the clubrooms when Charlotte demanded them all into the centre of the field.

'Guys, what *was* that?' said Charlotte, fuming, as they gathered around. 'We're better than this.'

CJ couldn't look at her.

'We started with a 2–2 draw this season. Okay. Fine. We barely knew each other *plus* it was against Lenny and the Hammerheads,' said Charlotte. 'But then we backed it up with a 0–0 draw. And after that, a 1–0 loss. And today, another 0–0 draw. And we had two *huge* chances to score.'

Two huge chances that I stuffed up, thought CJ, feeling Charlotte's eyes on him. But it wasn't just *her* glaring at CJ. Almost ALL his teammates' eyes darted over at him, before looking away. They were all thinking the same thing. HE'D LET THEM DOWN.

'Look, we just need to work harder, okay?' said Charlotte. Then she sighed. 'Come on. Let's get out of this tornado.'

Charlotte caught up to CJ as they headed for the visitors' clubrooms. 'Maybe some extra goal shooting practice for you this week? We need to be able to trust our star striker!'

'Sure,' said CJ. But he knew that wouldn't help. His miss-kicks weren't just bad luck or poor prep. It was more than that.

CJ had a **BIG PROBLEM** that no-one knew about. And he had no idea how to fix it.

CHAPTER TWO

PRANKS AND POINTERS

It was PRANK TIME.

Otherwise known as Sunday, 10.13 am.

The Jets were finishing up an EMERGENCY training session that Charlotte had called as everyone was leaving yesterday's match. CJ thought an **EMERGENCY** training session sounded like too much hard work so he'd suggested it be held at Jindaberg Beach. There were **NO COMPLAINTS**. Except from Charlotte. But they were meant to be co-captains, so CJ was glad that she backed down on this one. Plus, at the time, everyone was super keen to agree on a plan to get off the windy pitch after the contents of a garbage bin had blown all over them.

Fortunately, the wind had died down overnight and the morning's football practice had been a welcome change of scenery. As the session drew to a close, Charlotte gathered all the puffing, sweaty Jets together and used a stick to draw a mini football pitch in the sand. With everyone's eyes down, Benji gave CJ a wink and snuck away. He'd borrowed one of his father's precious homemade costumes from the Jindaberg Drama Club and was moments away from using it. Although probably not quite in a way his dad would've approved.

'Thanks again for coming along, everyone,' said Charlotte. 'Sorry we haven't had a chance to have a swim yet, Paul.'

'Hmmf,' replied the Paulveriser – a larger lad – who'd turned up wearing bright yellow Budgy Smugglers. What was the word CJ's mum would have used to describe it if she'd still been around? *Unflattering*. That's right. The look was UTTERLY *unflattering*.

Charlotte checked her watch, 'Okay. Before we finish up, we have just enough time to go through yesterday's missed goals.'

Do we have to? thought CJ. *I'd rather sit on an echidna . . . Nude.*

'Imagine this dead crab is Lexi.' Charlotte plonked the crab on the sand.

'Eww. I do NOT wanna be a dead crab!' squealed Lexi, then patted her cheeks. 'I think you'll find this skin is *anything* but crab-like.'

'Hey, I don't think it's dead!' laughed CJ, as the crab walked sideways across the six-yard box. 'Could've used him yesterday.'

'Might've been a straighter kick,' said Saanvi, as she shot a look at CJ.

That shut CJ up. Especially given Saanvi probably wasn't the only one thinking it.

CJ took a step away from the group and glanced around, wondering if Benji was in position for the prank. CJ couldn't see him. That was a good sign.

Charlotte began drawing arrows on the pitch between the sea objects, 'Okay, so this brown seaweed is CJ.'

'Double eww,' said Lexi, holding her nose. 'I think CJ is doggie doo.'

Seems about right, thought CJ.

Either way, Charlotte started explaining where they'd gone wrong. Antonio, Fahad,

May and all the other players listened intently. Charlotte's thoughts tumbled out her mouth. Clearly, she'd analysed the game **A HUNDRED DIFFERENT WAYS** the night before, in between her many family duties and strict homework schedule.

As Charlotte drew a long line towards the pier, CJ and the other Jets' eyes were drawn to the water. Morning light danced on the waves lapping at the shore.

Charlotte sighed. Only CJ noticed. The other Jets were too busy either checking out the water, soaking up the sun, or in the Paulveriser's case, adjusting his wedgie.

'Sorry, Charlotte, but maybe that's enough for today, yeah?' said CJ.

'Okay. Fine,' agreed Charlotte, checking her watch again. 'I'm due back home in seven minutes to mow the lawn anyway.'

But before that, it was time for CJ's part of Benji's cunning plan. Here goes . . . 'So, um. Why don't we all cool off with a bit of a swim, hey?'

'Yeah!'

'Good call, CJ!'

'Sweet!'

'Out of my way! I'm cannonballing off the jetty,' yelled the Paulveriser, stomping through the sand.

'Nice!' sniggered CJ. It was all falling into place.

The Jets left CJ and Charlotte behind on the beach, cheering as they all chased after the Paulveriser along the pier. 'Last one in is a rotten egg!'

There was no mistaking the first one in . . .

SPLOOOOOOSH!

The Paulveriser crashed into the water sending gallons of spray back up onto the pier. Then the other Jets jumped in after him. There were splashes everywhere.

'So, *this* is your contribution to our training session, is it?' asked Charlotte, arms crossed. 'Suggesting everyone does cannonballs –'

Then someone screamed, 'SHAAAARK!'

'What?!' shrieked Charlotte, yanking CJ's arm, dragging him to the edge of the water for a closer look.

'SHAAAAAARK!' cried Antonio, as he and the other Jets splashed around furiously beside the pier. White water flew in all directions. CJ glimpsed a fin.

Then the Paulveriser stuck his head out of the water and bawled, 'Help! I'm like a human happy meal, here!'

The Jets swam for the shore. Their arms and legs **CRASHING** through the water.

As CJ waited on the beach, Charlotte bolted into the water. She desperately helped her teammates onto the sand, dragging them to safety. In seconds, most were on the beach.

Then the Paulveriser called out from behind the waves! 'I'm stuck! Help!'

The fin popped in and out of the water nearby. 'Whoa, that looks super spooky,' said CJ.

'Paul's beached himself, we've got to do something!' said Charlotte, grabbing the football and **BOOTING** it hard in the direction of the shark.

WHACK!

The ball smacked into the grey shape. But Charlotte was too busy rolling the Paulveriser away from danger to check what she'd hit.

A wave pushed the shape closer to shore.

It emerged from the waves. Unsteady. Water cascaded down its sides.

'A walking shark!' gasped Lexi. 'This'll go viral. Let me get my iPad!'

As the falling water became just a trickle, all that was revealed underneath was a scrawny kid wearing a sopping wet grey onesie. A shark costume onesie. And a very lame one at that.

CJ burst out laughing.

Benji poked his head out of the costume. 'Gotcha!'

The Jets, who were catching their breath on the beach, quickly pieced it all together. A few laughed. Others rolled their eyes. The Paulveriser looked keen to take a shark bite out of Benji himself, but was puffing too hard to move.

'What is *wrong* with you two?' yelled Charlotte.

'Just a prank, dude,' said Benji, shaking water off like a dog.

'The un-funniest prank I've EVER seen,' snapped Charlotte, ripping Benji's shark head off and slamming it into the sand.

'Come on, we were just mucking around,' said CJ. 'You're only cracking it cos we gotcha good! It was hilarious!'

'Classic!' laughed Benji.

'Yeah, *real* funny. I thought my friends were in danger!' Charlotte sighed, then something occurred to her. 'No wonder neither of you were focused during training.'

'Come on, don't get your knickers in a pot,' said CJ.

'You mean KNOT!' yelled Charlotte. 'I'm sick of this. And I'm not alone. Highpants is

24

freaking out too! So, start taking football seriously or we'll never shake this losing streak. That goes for **EVERYONE!**'

The other Jets didn't dare meet Charlotte's eyes, but a few looked at CJ. They were miffed at the prank and seemed to blame him for being the one who sent them into the water.

Charlotte checked her watch. 'This afternoon I'm setting aside seventeen and a half minutes to rethink our *whole* approach. And make no mistake . . . things are going to change. **BIG TIME.**'

Charlotte grabbed her bag and stormed off.

Lexi whispered to CJ, 'I'm more scared now than when I thought there was a shark chasing me.'

'Think I'd prefer a shark,' said CJ.

FOOTBALL FUN FACTS – Winning and Losing Streaks

⚽ Sunderland A.F.C. holds the record for the longest losing streak in English Premier League (EPL) history. In 2002/03 they lost 15 games in a row. Ouch.

⚽ The longest winning streak in the EPL (so far) was achieved by Manchester City in 2017. The Sky Blues recorded 18 victories in a row.

⚽ The longest winning streak in the Hyundai A-League (so far) was achieved by the Western Sydney Wanderers in 2013. They recorded 10 victories in a row. Woohoo!

Facts checked and double-checked by Charlotte Alessi.

CHAPTER THREE

BOOMERANG BOOT

CJ and Benji decided to walk home via school to practise some penalties. And also so that CJ could avoid Charlotte, given his neighbour's current mood was set to NUCLEAR.

Garlic – the school gardener's dog – sat in goal. CJ and Benji took shots. Garlic made a half decent goalie; he just wasn't great at giving the balls back, so the Paulveriser's spot in the team was safe for now, despite probably having more fleas.

Benji had scored three from three. CJ hadn't managed one just yet. He fired off his fourth shot and it curved like a banana, **WAY OFF** target. It was more like a boomerang because it bounced back to him.

'Sweet. That's not easy to do,' said Benji.

'Didn't mean it,' said CJ with a sigh. Was his kicking getting worse? He needed a distraction. 'Give me one of your top five lists, Benji. Make it **TOP FIVE THINGS I'D RATHER DO THAN GIVE UP PRANKING.**'

'Okay dude, here we go:

1) Feed myself to an *actual* shark. I'd even make sure I was marinated.

2) Attend a live performance of Lexi reciting her poems about One Direction and their promising solo careers.

3) Pull out my nostril hair with a clamp / Pull out Highpants' nostril hair with a clamp. NB Would need to be a **VERY** sturdy clamp.

4) Eat just the mouldy bits from a piece of blue cheese . . . that'd been licked by our canine friend, Garlic.

5) Hand wash the Paulveriser's Budgy Smugglers.'

CJ giggled. Then missed **ANOTHER** penalty. That was enough football practice for now.

Once they convinced Garlic not to follow them, the two boys walked to Benji's dad's newsagency, barely a minute from school. They lingered out the front as Benji tried to squish the sopping wet shark costume further into his sports bag. Water dripped everywhere. CJ tried ramming his foot into the bag, but slipped, toppled backwards and smacked into the newsagency's front window.

OOOOF!

CJ's face ended up squished against a poster for the latest *Football Weekly Magazine*. The headline read, **TOMI JURIC'S GOLDEN BOOT!**

CJ used to have a golden boot too. Just like Socceroo star Tomi Juric. But not anymore. He sighed. Then he noticed the overgrown grass beside the newsagency. It was moving. There had to be something lurking in the gap between the buildings. Maybe something **DANGEROUS!**

CJ grinned. 'Sweet!' This was going to be interesting!

But Benji yanked him back behind the bins. 'Dude, nothing *sweet* would be hiding round there.'

Then the Paulveriser and Lenny Lincoln, the Jets' former captain, emerged from the gap.

Benji was right. There was nothing *sweet* about those two.

The Paulveriser and Lenny were still very good friends. Or very **BAD** friends, really, depending how you looked at it.

The boys squeezed their way out to get to the footpath. The Paulversier was as round as a beach ball and Lenny was the shape of a gorilla, if it weren't for his mohawk.

Lenny dusted leaves off his tank top. 'Best thing is, we've still got another one kilo bag of lollies left! Nice. No-one will ever find 'em back there! Ha! Always been the perfect hiding spot.'

The Paulveriser grunted his approval as he chewed, with little dollops of drool and lolly snake tumbling from his mouth. Then CJ noticed the pattern on the Paulveriser's T-shirt was actually just bits of gooey lollies that had fallen and gotten stuck.

'Here we go,' whispered Benji.

CJ tensed up, preparing himself for another not-so-fun confrontation with his ex-teammate, but Lenny and the Paulveriser turned away and started walking. They hadn't noticed CJ and Benji beside the bins.

'Let's head to the quarry. Smash some rocks!' said Lenny.

The Paulveriser grunted again.

Lenny seemed to understand. 'Yep. Donut shop on the way, man.'

PHEW!

CJ didn't need **ANOTHER** run-in right now. Not after Charlotte's wobbly on the beach.

'We'll catch up with those two another time then?' whispered Benji, moving from behind the bins.

'Can't wait,' replied CJ.

'Okay, dude. I better sneak Dad's shark costume back into the storeroom where he keeps all the Drama Club stuff. Catch ya later.'

'Cool. Oh, and nice pranking, partner!' CJ gave his best friend a high five. Benji's bag continued dripping as he entered the newsagency.

But no matter how effective Benji's prank was, CJ still had that empty feeling gnawing at the pit of his stomach. Had he lost his goal scoring ability for good?

CHAPTER FOUR

THE WHIFF FACTOR

CJ was in no hurry to get home. He killed some time making **RUDE SHADOW PUPPETS** on the local café's awnings. He got quite a few toots and thumbs up from passing cars for his work. But when the café owner finally noticed, and dropped a plate of jam and scones on an old lady, CJ thought it was best to move on.

CJ's mouth went dry as he rounded the corner to his street. He spotted Charlotte in her front yard. She was kicking to herself using her trusty football on a totem pole device. She had a **HUGE PILE** of books open on the grass. Pure Charlotte: **EXTREME MULTI-TASKING.**

CJ whirled back around. He decided to try some more shadow puppetry.

'CJ!' called Charlotte.

CJ froze. He turned back. 'Oh, hey!'

'We need to talk. ASAP. Get over here.'

CJ considered miming being taken by a tornado. But the wind had died down since yesterday, so perhaps it wouldn't be 100 per cent believable.

As he got closer he listened in awe to Charlotte's kicking and studying routine . . .

'Hydrogen.'

SMACK! She thumped the football.

'Helium.'

SMACK!

'Lithium.'

SMACK!

'What's next, what's next?' wondered Charlotte, frustrated.

'Um, gymnasium?' suggested CJ.

Charlotte didn't kick the ball. She just stared at CJ. 'Sometimes I'm certain that you must *practise* being a dingbat.'

'I take that as a compliment,' said CJ, as he turned to leave. 'Okay. *Later!*'

'Don't move,' said Charlotte, grabbing his shoulder. 'I'm still spewing about the dumb stunt you and Benji pulled at the beach.'

'Yeah. Thought you might be.'

'However, after thinking it over, I've decided I'm going to overlook it,' said Charlotte, releasing a long calming breath. 'Because as your co-captain, I have to ask you something. What's up with you at the moment? Tell me. *Now.*'

'Huh?' asked CJ, playing dumb, but Charlotte tilted her head and used her 'don't mess with me eyes'. They were as deadly as Mile Jedinak in front of goal.

CJ sighed. 'Fine. But this is top-secret, okay? I haven't even told Benji.'

Charlotte's expression softened. 'Cross my heart.'

'Cos I wouldn't want to look stupid in front of all the others.'

'I wouldn't worry about that,' said Charlotte. 'Tell me.'

'It's my special gold boots. The ones covered in glitter that glow in the dark. You know the ones?'

'Know them? They should come with warnings, like staring at an eclipse.'

'Well, no need to worry now because they're gone. I've been wearing op shop replacements. Nowhere near as special as my originals.'

'Come on, CJ. Boots are boots. How special could they be?'

'It's a long story.'

Charlotte checked her watch. 'I have three minutes, thirteen seconds.'

'I'll speak fast. Let me take you back to a time many years ago . . .'

If this was a TV show – here's where the screen would go all wibbly-wobbly and there'd be hypnotic harp music. Yes, it was time for a FLASHBACK . . .

It was 2012. At five years old, CJ was attending his **FIRST EVER** Socceroos match. It was a present from his mum, before she got sick. It was one of those presents that seemed to be just as much for the giver as the receiver, because CJ's mum was as **PUMPED** as he was. She'd put streaks of green through her blonde hair and made them both matching T-shirts. When they stood side by side the T-shirts spelt out 'BRAZIL OR BUST!'

The game was a World Cup Qualifier, in preparation for Brazil 2014.

Australia versus Saudi Arabia. AAMI Park. **SELL OUT.** 24,000 plus!

The Socceroos were down 2–1 at half-time. Even as a youngster, CJ was **OBSESSED** with football. He was jiggling his legs in his seat, worried for the team. The Aussies needed to pull out something special. CJ stood, trying to shake off his nerves.

That was when CJ's mum grabbed his hand. She squeezed it. Twice. That had always been their secret signal to say, 'I'm thinking of you.' Whenever they were out and about and he and his mum were holding hands, if she gave him two quick squeezes, nothing needed to be said. And it always made him feel warmer inside.

CJ sat back down. His mum smiled. 'Relax. Just like you, CJ, the Socceroos don't know *how* to give up.'

She was right. In the second half the Aussies kicked THREE GOALS IN THREE MINUTES. Including one off the boot of the legendary Harry Kewell. They won the game 4–2. Little CJ sprayed his soft drink into the air and his mum had to grab him to stop him jumping the fence to celebrate.

Soon after the final whistle, superstar midfielder James Troisi came over to sign autographs for fans. A pair of football boots got thrown to him to sign. They were VERY gold and VERY sparkly. Troisi signed them, but couldn't find the owners in the crowd, so he just handed them straight to CJ.

Once home, CJ stuffed the toes with tissue paper so he could wear the boots in his first ever game for the Jets: the Under 6's.

'. . . And wearing those boots I kicked the very first goal for the Jets,' said CJ, back in the present day.

'Whoa. And you've worn them ever since?'

'Uh-huh. They're my secret weapon. Make me kick straight. Troisi magic!'

'Magic boots?' Charlotte raised her eyebrows. 'This another stupid prank?'

CJ shook his head.

Charlotte sighed. 'Right. Well, we could use a bit more *magic* in the forward line on Saturday.'

'Agreed. But my magic boots have disappeared. Maybe even gone FOREVER! And I haven't been able to kick a single goal since I lost them.'

CJ was relieved to get his secret off his chest. Even if Charlotte thought he was TOTALLY NUTS, at least one person in the team now knew why he was playing so bad.

With honesty time over, CJ was never one to mope around – also he felt pretty silly about the whole magic boot story – so he started jumping about and shadow boxing the totem pole. Then he tried to boot Charlotte's football that was hanging from the pole. He gave it everything he had.

CLAAAAAANG!

His toe SMACKED into the pole.

'Ow! Ow! Ow!' yelped CJ, jumping on one foot. 'See? What did I tell you? The magic boots really do help me kick. You've gotta believe me!'

'I believe that *you* think that's what they do,' said Charlotte.

CJ didn't follow that, but he appreciated the way Charlotte looked sort of like she cared. It made a nice change from her looking at him like he was a **WART** of some kind. She checked her watch, but then as if to say 'screw it', she walked them over to the front wall and they sat up against it, like they used to do when they were younger. As kids they used to sit there for hours talking about playing for Australia one day.

'Okay. If this will help the team, I'll help you,' said Charlotte. 'When was the last time you saw your so called *magic boots*? We need to get them back.'

'Straight after the first game of the season against the Hammerheads,' said CJ, picturing

45

taking off his boots in the clubrooms during the celebrations. 'But when I got home my boots weren't in my bag.'

Charlotte had a faraway look. 'If there was a mix-up and another teammate took your boots by mistake, you'd think they would've said something by now. I mean, they're hard to miss. Maybe we should make an announcement just in case –'

'No. Magic boots are kind of . . . embarrassing. Can we just keep this between us?'

Charlotte glanced CJ up and down. 'Sure. You know, you're an *okay* guy when you're not in crazy CJ mode.'

CJ grinned. 'Me? Crazy?'

'So, the way I see it, if we want you kicking straight again, we need to catch the thief.'

'Thief? Whoa! I'd never thought of that! Oh, oh, I know,' said CJ, jumping to his feet.

'Let's do one of Benji's top five things . . . We'll call it **TOP FIVE SUSPECTS WHO MAY HAVE STOLEN CJ'S MAGIC BOOTS**.

1) Highpants – stole the boots to strip them for their colourful material to further increase the length of his pants in new and exciting ways.

2) Benji – he's CJ's best friend so no-one would ever suspect him. But perhaps this was his plan all along. Since birth. Or even earlier.

3) Garlic the dog – might have been taught to fetch slippers for Baldock, but Garlic might've taken his training one step too far.

4) The Paulveriser – may have thought the sparkly shoes were large Ferrero Rochers and swallowed them both in one gulp.

5) Charlotte – jealous of CJ's incredible skill, popularity, and heroic braveness, Charlotte stole the boots for herself. Hopefully she likes toe jam.'

Charlotte sighed. 'If you think I'd put my feet near ANYTHING your stinky feet have been associated with, you must be dumber than you look.'

'I take that as a compliment,' said CJ. 'Hang on! Do my feet *really* smell?'

'Not just your feet. Your WHIFF FACTOR is through the roof. I keep thinking there's a gas leak!'

'What? Me?'

'It's like you wear fart scented deodorant.'

'But I shower every second week!'

'I rest my case,' said Charlotte. She glimpsed down at her watch. 'Look, I've got to go. Let's talk more about this tomorrow at school. By the way, try to stay on Highpants' good side for once. He's on edge – I heard him mumbling to himself yesterday. Blames himself for how the team's going, if you can believe that. Reckons his message isn't sinking in.'

'He has a *message*?'

'He thinks he's Graham Arnold. Look, I'll do you a deal, if you get serious this week, I'll help you get your *detective* on!'

'Thanks, co-captain! Deal,' said CJ, but it was difficult to concentrate on his co-captain duties when he knew one of his teammates, one of his friends even, was out to ruin him. He was playing alongside a BOOT THIEF! The more he thought about it, the more it ate him up inside. Friends, teammates, whatever . . . EVERYONE was a suspect!

CHAPTER FIVE

MUGSHOTS

It was Monday morning. CJ was late for school, as usual, and he was frantically searching the hallway cupboard for football boots he could use until he and Charlotte found his stolen magic boots. The ones he had been wearing from the op shop **SUCKED**. He hadn't kicked a single goal since he'd started wearing them. CJ hurled the entire contents of the cupboard onto the floor and found a great option.

His mum's old football boots! They were far too big for him, but all they needed was his standard trick of tissue paper stuffed into the toes. Except this time round he decided he'd use a clean tissue. **LESSON LEARNT!**

His mum's old boots looked kind of similar to his missing magic boots. They were also **VERY COLOURFUL**, with fluoro pink shoelaces that had yellow specks. Maybe CJ got his flair for boot fashion from his mum? These would do nicely.

When CJ rocked up to school – 30 minutes late – he was greeted by his entire class waiting outside the school's hall. That was weird . . .

UH–OH!

Today was school photos day! CJ had **COMPLETELY FORGOTTEN** about the photos and he'd turned up in his sports uniform. Which had a few holes. And a few stains.

'Typical,' muttered Highpants, as he looked CJ up and down. 'We'll have to hide you up the back. I just don't know what more I can do to get through to you kids these days!'

All CJ's classmates filed into the hall for their group shot. CJ found himself towards the end of a long platform that elevated the kids in the back row. Last year he'd sat next to Benji near the front, but after the faces they'd pulled, and a few parents' complaints, Principal Swift had ensured they were separated this time round.

The photographer – with thick-rimmed glasses and a man-bun – had his camera hooked up to a laptop. Everyone could see the picture as he was framing it up.

'Smile, children,' said Highpants. 'Or detentions all round.'

CJ wasn't smiling. He was distracted, staring at the various classmates from his football team, wondering who had stolen his magic boots. His eyes fell on Saanvi. She and CJ had never gotten along. Maybe she'd sabotaged him?

CLICK!

'No flash, sorry,' said the photographer, adjusting his camera settings. But even though the picture was dark, the kids could still see what the shot had looked like on the screen. CJ had been staring at Saanvi. His eyes narrow, mean and full of suspicion.

'CJ, eyes straight ahead this time,' said Highpants, his voice icy cold.

Right in front of CJ was Lexi. Maybe she was jealous of CJ's super skills? She loved attention, after all.

The photographer had another go.

CLICK!

CJ was caught giving Lexi an all-time filthy look. The expression stood out to everyone. The class laughed. Other than Lexi, who shot CJ an equally filthy look back and said. 'Jealous that the camera loves me, CJ?'

'We will *not* have a repeat of last year, Mr Jackson!' growled Highpants, developing a sweaty top lip. 'Smile! Or I will *make* you smile.'

Charlotte leaned over in front of Antonio and whispered to CJ. 'I wouldn't test him today, dingbat!'

But as they waited for the cameraman to get his flash working, CJ's suspicious mind kicked in again. He noticed Fahad. CJ once *accidently* copied Fahad's entire science homework – even Fahad's name! Maybe this was payback? CJ got up on one foot, leaning at 45 degrees, arms flapping, as he glared at Fahad, wondering if he was the thief.

'Stop it, CJ!' whispered Charlotte.

Right at that moment, CJ felt the platform wobble beneath him. Other kids felt it too. CJ shifted his weight but it was too late. The platform flung itself upwards. All of a sudden the back row lost their balance, throwing their arms up in the air as they were THRUST FORWARDS.

'WHOA! AUUGH! OOOF!'

They fell in a heap. Grade Five were all piled on top of each other. And just at that moment, the flash went off.

CLICK!

'Mr Jaaaackson!' roared Highpants, from somewhere in the middle of jumbled bodies.

UH–OH!

But this was all the wonky platform's fault! CJ was certain he wouldn't get in any real trouble for this one.

CJ spent his whole lunch break in detention. At least he was able to pass the time by bopping along to the drumbeats that were spilling out of Highpants' headphones, who was listening to music at his desk while he marked assignments. As CJ watched his teacher work, it occurred to him that Highpants must go through a LOT of red pens.

However, CJ's mood began to darken again the moment he spotted some of his teammates playing outside the classroom window. He couldn't help but continue to cast a suspicious eye over them all, even Benji. Maybe he'd need to interrogate each suspect at training on Wednesday. Thankfully with CJ *and* Charlotte's brains combined they almost had TWO WHOLE BRAINS on the case.

Someone was sure to CRACK.

CHAPTER SIX

LOW PANTS

On Wednesday arvo, CJ couldn't wait to get to training and try out his mum's football boots. But as he jogged up the hill to the pitch he stopped dead in his tracks . . .

'What the –'

Highpants was already there, in the centre of the field. For the first time ever, their teacher and coach, Highpants, was wearing jeans. That's right, actual DENIM. And they were hanging LOW. Plus, it looked like he had bling round his neck. WEIRDEST LOOK EVER.

But if that wasn't enough, the music teacher, Miss Harmon, was beside Highpants. Normally she wore long floral dresses, with her hair in a perfect bob and sung songs about rainbows and unicorns. Today she wore a cap backwards with tufts of hair sticking out the sides and oversized sunglasses that featured dollar signs. She was standing behind a deck of turntables and dramatically hit a button.

The drumbeat kicked in. Both teachers closed their eyes as they grooved.

'Yo!' hollered Highpants, as Benji and a few other Jets arrived on the pitch. 'Word!

I'm thinkin' you kids aren't feeling the love from the sideline songs I've been laying down this season. M'right?'

Highpants seemed to be attempting an American accent. Either that or he had a swollen tongue.

'Sorry, everyone. I'm thirty-seven seconds late,' said Charlotte, struggling up the hill with a string bag of extra footballs. CJ gave her a hand. Benji gave her a wide berth.

'You haven't missed much,' said CJ, pointing to Highpants.

'Ya'll gather round, Homers!'

'Homies!' Miss Harmon corrected Highpants. 'I think!'

'Homies! Cos today I'm speaking at you on *your* level. Got to get through to your little minds,' said Highpants, tapping the side of his bald head.

Alongside Charlotte, Lexi – who pretty much treated the Grade Five iPad as her own – started filming for her YouTube channel. Turns out Lexi's football updates got double the hits of her other posts. She reckoned that was because she was being so much more 'real'. Well, now it was time to capture the football team's *real* disgust.

Baldock, Jindaberg Primary's gardener, was attending to the cherry blossom tree near the playground as Highpants began his rap debut. Everyone knew him as Baldock, but CJ had no idea if that was his first name or his last. He was a big, round old bloke – unshaven and dirty, with dark lines around his eyes. He smelt almost as bad as his dog, Garlic, but despite this the only words CJ had ever heard Baldock croak out were, 'STINKY KIDS.' He wasn't the cheeriest of chaps.

As the music blared out across the grounds Baldock cringed and covered his ears with his huge, filthy hands. Garlic, on the other hand, jumped about and howled along to the music. It was all getting too much for Baldock. He flung his arms in the air, gesturing for Highpants to pull the plug. No luck.

CJ began to wonder if he was as stinky as Baldock. The problem was that if CJ didn't wash his hair for a month, it would stay positioned just the way he liked it. And he didn't want to give that up.

Highpants began his rap. 'THE JETS, YO! WE'RE THE BEST, YO! WE PLAY WITH YO—YOS!'

'Freestyling isn't his thing,' laughed Benji.

'I LIKE TALKIN' HISTORY, SO IT'S NO MYSTERY, THAT THE JETS DO THIS TO ME . . .'

Highpants mimed his mind being blown.

'. . . WHEN THEY GET ON THE GRASS!'

Lexi gave the iPad camera a baffled look.

'SO WATCH OUT PRETENDERS, YOU'LL NEVER BEND US, WHEREVER THEY SEND US, YOU CAN KISS MY —'

FZZZT! KLUNK!

Baldock had pulled a lever inside the power box that was mounted on the side of the clubrooms. He'd cut the power. The Jets cheered.

'Well, besties, ciao for now. That's just another crazy day playing for the Jets! See ya!' said Lexi, blowing a kiss into her iPad as she finished her recording.

'Hang on,' said Charlotte, taking the iPad from Lexi. 'When did you start recording your Jets videos?'

'After our first game of the year. It was super exciting in the clubrooms. I had so much to say that I think I was the last to leave!'

CJ noticed Benji move further away from Charlotte. His cap was pulled down and it was weird to see him without his cheeky grin.

'Did you hear that, CJ?' asked Charlotte.

'Um, sweet,' said CJ. He wasn't sure why Charlotte was so interested in Lexi's videos all of a sudden. The Jets were meant to be getting stuck into training, which Charlotte had been talking about **NON STOP** since their last training session.

'Let's do this!' said CJ, kicking a football to himself. But Charlotte stayed put.

'You mean, you recorded footage from *after* the game?' asked Charlotte.

'Uh-huh,' Lexi said. 'Three thousand likes and counting.'

'Could we see that footage?' asked Charlotte.

Lexi tapped the iPad, selecting the video files folder. Hundreds of icons appeared. Every file had a different background, but each showed Lexi smiling her killer smile.

Charlotte took CJ aside, 'CJ, do you know what this means?'

CJ shrugged. 'Probably not.'

'We may have footage of the boot thief,' exclaimed Charlotte, grabbing CJ's hands. 'We're about to discover who stole your magic boots!'

CJ's eyes went wide. The mystery was about to be **SOLVED!**

FOOTBALL FUN FACTS - Football Boots

⚽ The first pair of football boots in recorded history were owned by King Henry VIII of England.

⚽ The founders of the two largest football boot companies in the world were actually brothers. Adolf Dassler was behind Adidas and Rudolf Dassler founded Puma.

⚽ One particular pair of football boots, signed by former England captain Steven Gerrard, sold for over $71,000 in 2015. The money raised was donated to the British Red Cross Refugee Appeal.

Facts checked and double-checked by Charlotte Alessi.

CHAPTER SEVEN

DEFECTIVE DETECTIVES

Highpants was clearly miffed that Baldock ruined his rap. But no-one messed with Baldock. Instead, Highpants put down his mic and called all the Jets together. It was hard to tell if he was more **SWEATY OR ANGRY**.

'Highpants is about to go ballistic. Let's check the iPad footage straight after training,' said Charlotte to CJ. 'We'll find the boot thief, but right now we've got to be co-captains and focus on the team.'

'Children, children, children,' sneered Highpants, pulling up his low hanging jeans and accidently exposing his My Little Pony socks. 'So far your season has been disappointing . . . to say the least. Despite all my efforts, you have not won a single game.'

'We just need to get serious. In my heart of hearts I know we can do better,' agreed Charlotte.

Benji nudged CJ. They both cracked up laughing. Charlotte glared at them. Benji looked away, muffling his mouth. CJ felt he should explain. 'Sorry. It's just that it sounded like you said "heart of farts".'

Charlotte grit her teeth. 'Heart . . . Of . . . Hearts.'

Highpants loomed over them. 'Here's a tip, lads. If *you* don't take yourself seriously, no-one else will.'

Then Benji spoke up to Highpants, which almost never happened. 'Hang on. Isn't football meant to be fun?'

Highpants GLARED. CJ looked to Charlotte. In fact all the Jets looked to Charlotte, wondering who she was going to side with.

Charlotte glanced back at them all. 'I agree with the coach. Let's get serious.'

Highpants grinned. His teeth seemed somehow brighter than his fake bling.

The Jets dragged their feet as they dumped their bags in the clubrooms then returned to the pitch for some drills. CJ got everyone to split up in to smaller groups for dribbling practice. Benji seemed to be getting better every day. He could kick on both sides, plus he was light on his feet, able to keep upright when the ball was being contested. All those years as the Jets mascot, where he would perform amazing gymnastics moves, were now paying off. Benji was BEAMING with delight. Except when Highpants came over to check on their progress. Benji immediately got nervous and started stuffing up.

'Focus, Benji!' said Highpants.

CJ glanced around at his teammates. Any one of them could be the boot thief. Pretending he was practising making a wall to block a free kick in defence, CJ took the opportunity to gather all his teammates at the top of the square. He created a good old-fashioned line-up of suspects, just like in the movies.

CJ took his time walking from one end of the line to the other. Every so often he slowed to get right up in one of his teammate's faces, but he regretted getting so close to the Paulveriser when the big guy let out a deafening BUUUUUUURP!

Charlotte stepped out from the line-up to stand beside CJ. She looked like she was about to suggest another drill when CJ addressed the group. 'You know where I think we're going wrong, Jets?'

'Where, CJ? Do tell,' said Saanvi, arms crossed.

'No trust.'

'Is this necessary?' whispered Charlotte. 'We have the iPad footage.'

CJ searched their faces. He wanted to give the thief an opportunity to confess, but he didn't want to get into the whole 'I used to have magic boots' thing.

73

'We're meant to be a team, after all! But one of you has let me down. Whoever you are, I hope you understand what I'm imploding.'

'Imploding? Sure you don't mean *implying*?' suggested Charlotte.

'Both,' said CJ, trying to look tough. No-one confessed. Most looked confused or offended, or both.

Charlotte quickly suggested they practise the Jets' latest set play – STINKY NAPPY. She sent CJ off to the clubrooms to grab some witches hats. While they waited CJ noticed her handing everyone seven sheets of paper stapled together. She called it a FUN FOOTBALL QUIZ! But the Paulveriser perfectly summed up the mood of the team.

'This SUCKS!' he declared, with an upturned lip.

Once inside the clubrooms, CJ spotted the iPad sticking out of Lexi's bag. He scrolled through all the files until he found the video he needed. He hit **PLAY**. Lexi banged on about the first game of the season. She was standing in the middle of the room, but over her shoulder CJ saw himself. He was spraying a sports drink over Benji. **HILARIOUS!** As Lexi talked and talked and then talked some more, including detailing the various stages her hair went through during the match, CJ kept his eyes on the background. The magic boots remained resting against his sports bag.

Plenty of players walked through the shot. A few even danced. Saanvi, Antonio, May, the Paulveriser, Charlotte and a whole heap more. He just had to wait till one of them grabbed the shoes. It went on and on. People started to leave. CJ got bored. He pressed fast-forward. No-one was stealing the magic boots. Then he saw himself grabbing his bag and leaving the clubrooms with Charlotte. **HE'D LEFT THE BOOTS BEHIND!**

On screen, Lexi kept talking to the camera as she followed the others out of the clubrooms. She was the last to leave. Her video clip continued all the way home, till she reached her house.

CJ sighed. There was **NO FOOTAGE** of a thief in action. He'd left his magic boots behind, but where were they now? He'd already checked Principal Swift's lost property box.

He double-checked that the boots weren't under the bench. They weren't in the locker either. So, whoever took his boots did it *after* the Jets had left that day. CJ's tummy flipped. Maybe he was wrong to suspect his teammates after all?

Then he heard Charlotte calling. 'CJ, stop messing around! We need you out here!'

CJ gave up on the iPad, grabbed the witches hats and bolted out the door. As he ran through the exit, he almost collided with Baldock who was pruning some hedges.

'Stinky kid,' muttered Baldock, as Garlic jumped up onto CJ for a pat.

'Not now, mate.'

After training everyone started packing up their stuff in the clubrooms, but Highpants called CJ and Charlotte outside for a chat. CJ felt the wet grass ooze up through his football socks. He'd taken off his mother's boots because the tissue paper solution wasn't as comfortable as he'd remembered.

'I'm sure I don't have to remind you, but Saturday's game occurs during the school fete.'

Charlotte nodded. 'I know, I'm making biscotti for the cake stall.'

'Me too,' said CJ, lying. He'd forgotten all about the fete, and wasn't quite sure what biscotti was.

'The Jets football team will be on show,' said Highpants, as CJ and Charlotte waved off

Lexi, Saanvi, Fahad and the other Jets as they left the pitch. None of them seemed all that cheery to their co-captains. Plus, it appeared CJ's arch rival, Lenny, had arrived to meet the Paulveriser, as they were both walking past too. Behind Highpants, Lenny lunged in CJ's direction and made a silent RARR! CJ didn't budge.

'Are you paying attention, Mr Jackson? The whole suburb will be watching this Saturday, so you and your prankster pal better be one hundred per cent focused or else,' warned Highpants, locking eyes with CJ for an uncomfortably long time before turning to help Miss Harmon pack up the turntables.

SNIFF.

'Eww, stinky.' Charlotte looked down and noticed CJ was shoeless. 'Oh no! We forgot to check Lexi's video.'

'Nope. I checked it myself.'

'Oh, great. And?'

'And the video makes it pretty clear, I left my magic boots behind in the clubrooms after our first game. Every Jet left the room empty-handed. So it's possible that it wasn't a teammate who stole my boots after all.'

Charlotte screwed up her forehead. 'I'm kind of relieved, but that doesn't really help us. I mean, who goes into the clubrooms apart from us?'

Just then, CJ and Charlotte both noticed Baldock, limping over to the clubroom doors jingling his big set of school keys.

'Wow, I'm a genius! I think I've solved it,' said CJ. 'By a pretty clever process of illumination.'

'Elimination.'

'It has to be Baldock. He locks up the rooms. He must have seen my boots and stolen them.'

'But why?'

'Dunno. Souvenir from a legend?' CJ pointed to himself.

'He probably turfed them out because of their rancid smell.'

CJ leaned forward to sniff the air above his socks. *Yep. A little ripe. Maybe Charlotte was right.* Then it occurred to him that he'd left his mum's boots inside the clubrooms, right now. **UNPROTECTED.** 'Whatever the reason, Baldock's about to steal another pair!'

'Go!' yelled Charlotte.

CJ bolted over to the clubrooms, 'Freeze, Baldock!' His mind was fixed on his mum's boots rather than just how scary Baldock was. 'Stay away from my mum's football boots!'

CHAPTER EIGHT

PARMESAN ON POOP

'Stop right there!' cried CJ, arriving at the clubroom doors just as Baldock was about to shuffle inside.

Baldock grunted, as if to say 'cool it, kid,' but CJ pushed past him and got inside. He jumped

up on the bench with his palms raised trying to freeze the moment.

'Don't move an inch, boot thief!'

Baldock ignored him and started turning off the lights.

'I said STOP!'

Baldock paused. He grumbled to himself and shook his head.

'I'm onto you,' said CJ, turning to point to where he'd left his stuff. 'I'm not going to fall for this twice. I know you've come in here to steal my boots.'

'What boots?' asked Charlotte from the doorway.

Huh? CJ glanced down at the bench. She was right. There *were* **NO BOOTS**. CJ's bag was open, lying on its side, and the boots were already gone.

'But? Wha? Um.' CJ wasn't making much sense as he jumped down and double-checked that his mum's boots were definitely missing.

Charlotte ran over and looked under the bench. Then she opened all the lockers. She also jumped up to glance along the top of the lockers where the windows met the ceiling. She even peered into the rubbish bin. No boots anywhere.

KLUNK! KLUNK! Baldock thumped his key change into the lights' switch. He stared at CJ and Charlotte.

'He wants to lock up,' said CJ.

'Lucky that's all he wants,' replied Charlotte. 'After *your* accusations.'

CJ and Charlotte grabbed their bags. They hurried out of the clubrooms as Baldock started flicking off the last couple of lights.

A second later, CJ poked his head back in, 'Um, sorry!'

Baldock grunted. CJ zipped out of there.

Outside, Charlotte suggested they scan their surroundings for clues. She checked the Captain Jindaberg statue.

'Nothing.'

CJ shook the cherry blossom tree. 'Still nothing!'

Charlotte gave the playground a once over. 'More nothing!'

CJ even ventured into the chicken coop. The featherless chicken EYED HIM OFF. The others waddled towards him. Even though he took a quick look he was pretty sure none of them were using his mum's old boots as a nest. Of course, doing so would've required a rather uniquely shaped butt.

'Big fat zero,' said CJ. 'Normal butt chickens.'

'What?'

'Don't worry.'

Charlotte explained that she'd scheduled herself to finish some maths homework, put out the bins and repair her brother's BMX before she cooked dinner for the family. CJ's schedule wasn't quite as full, but they got moving regardless.

Garlic bounded up to them at the school gate. CJ gave the scruffy dog a big pat. 'You seriously reckon my socks smell worse than *this* guy.'

'A real toss up,' said Charlotte. 'Hang on. Wow! That's given me a brilliant idea.'

CJ winked. 'You're welcome!'

'You stink!'

'Hey!'

'Like parmesan on poop, or something. But let's use that!' said Charlotte, clapping her hands together. 'Take one of your socks off and let Garlic have a good sniff. He might be able to track down your mum's boots.'

'Aw, yeah! Sweet!' said CJ, yanking off his sock and waving it in the air like it was some sort of dog treat.

'Not so close to *me*,' said Charlotte, holding her nose and shoving CJ away.

Garlic wagged his tail. He had the sock's scent and he was off.

CJ and Charlotte sprinted after Garlic, straight through the school gates and up the street. With CJ dribbling a football at his feet, they weaved through parked bikes, wheelie bins and adults drinking their chai lattes outside the café that CJ had recently been banned from. CJ felt like Aaron Mooy weaving through opposition defenders for the Socceroos.

All of a sudden Garlic stopped. CJ too. Charlotte slammed into CJ. Garlic barked. They were on a street corner, standing in front of a post office box, just outside the donut store.

'Has someone mailed the boots somewhere?' wondered CJ, before getting down on one knee. 'What is it, boy? Where are the boots?'

Garlic twitched his nose and he was off again. CJ kicked the football to Charlotte and this time she dribbled as they veered into the park, straight through a group of people presenting a giant chocolate birthday cake to a chubby five-year-old boy. CJ tried to half apologise by singing along to 'Happy Birthday', but couldn't help busting out the 'you look like a monkey' version and grabbing a stack of fairy bread as he sprinted through.

'Sorry about him, it's a FOOTBALL EMERGENCY!' called Charlotte, as she hurried after CJ.

They jumped a narrow creek – Charlotte used some superb foot-juggling skills – and ended up ducking through an empty block that led to one of Jindaberg's back streets. Dump trucks filled with stone drove up and down the street and grit hung in the air.

Garlic came to another abrupt stop at the local tip, opposite the entrance to the quarry. Charlotte fanned her nose to fight off the smell of rubbish.

CJ watched Garlic scratch himself behind the ear.

'I'm not seeing your boots,' said Charlotte. 'All this tells us is that your feet smell like the local tip.'

CJ scanned the grassy footpath, then peered through the tip fence. Even he found the smell unpleasant.

Garlic just kept scratching himself. If he was ever actually following the scent in the first place, he seemed to have COMPLETELY lost it now.

'Keep it up, wonderdog,' said CJ with a sigh. He'd thought Charlotte might've been onto something with this idea.

Charlotte shrugged, then checked her watch. 'Sorry, CJ. I've got to get going.'

'Yeah, fair enough.'

Charlotte started walking, but then she stopped. She looked down at the grass, then crouched. CJ ran over. It wasn't his stolen boots, but it *was* a shoelace. A fluoro pink shoelace, with yellow specks. It had to be from his mum's boots.

CJ's eyes darted around the ground. There was nothing else. Just grass and dirt.

As Garlic rolled around in mud, CJ ran the shoelace through his fingers. Did it mean anything that it had been found near the tip? In a way, letting his mum's boots get stolen was even worse than losing his magic boots in the first place. Perhaps he'd never find either of them.

It may have been a stupid superstition, but it worked. CJ was terrified that without his magic boots he might not kick a goal ever again. If so, the Jets were in trouble. And CJ's football career may as well be **OVER**.

FOOTBALL FUN FACTS - Superstitions

⚽ Brazilian legend Pelé once gave a match
  shirt to a fan, only to suffer a performance
  slump. Once the shirt was returned, Pelé was
  suddenly back to his best. (No-one told Pelé
  it wasn't the same shirt!)

⚽ Westfield Matildas star Steph Catley got
  herself into the habit of always being the
  last one on the pitch for training. She also
  eats her mum's spaghetti bolognese before
  home games. Yum.

⚽ France won the 1998 World Cup and one of
  their rituals was to listen to Gloria Gaynor's
  1970s hit 'I Will Survive' in the change room.

Facts checked and double-checked by
Charlotte Alessi.

CHAPTER NINE

BOBÔ AND BARBAROUSES

As Grade Five shuffled into class on Thursday morning, CJ noticed that none of the Jets were talking to him, probably because of his weird behaviour at practice the night before. But lucky for him, most kids were distracted by the buzz in the air for the A-League match that night.

'Dude! You pumped for the game tonight? It's the Big Blue,' said Benji, sitting down beside CJ as Highpants began another one of his boring lessons. 'Lexi's getting a group together. She's got free tickets! We'll be able to see Bobô in action!'

'Much prefer to see *Barbarouses* in action! Sweet, I'm in,' said CJ.

'Shhhh!' whispered Charlotte, a few desks over, rolling her eyes at Benji.

Benji blew her a raspberry. 'She needs to get over herself.'

'Nah, she's cool,' said CJ, thinking about how helpful Charlotte had been in trying to track down his stolen boots.

But Benji wasn't listening. He handed CJ a note:

TOP FIVE REASONS CHARLOTTE NEEDS TO RELAX!

1) Any more straining and she'll give herself haemorrhoids. (Just ask my dad. But **NEVER** borrow his ointment.)

2) Too much thinking can turn you into a zombie. (Not scientifically proven but *something* must be causing all the zombie outbreaks.)

3) Getting stressed out will cause chickenpox. (Also not scientifically proven, but it's not worth risking becoming a zombie with chickenpox.)

4) If Charlotte pulls her ponytail any tighter her eyes will relocate to the top of her head.

5) She's becoming less popular than a zombiefied Highpants with chickenpox.

CJ smiled. But he wasn't exactly
Mr Popularity with the team either.

⚽

That night, Lexi's mum accompanied CJ, Benji,
Charlotte and Lexi to a bustling AAMI Park
for the Melbourne Victory vs Sydney FC game.
There were people EVERYWHERE. A sea of blue.

As they hurried towards the stairs, CJ and
his friends were greeted by a MASSIVE football.
There were arms and legs sticking out of it, and
also a head. The head belonged to Lexi's dad,
Mr Li. CJ had heard that Lexi's dad had been
crowned Mr New Zealand a few years ago, but
those days seemed to be behind him. Tonight
he was jumping around dressed as a giant
football. This must have been how Lexi got
the free tickets.

'Classic! Your dad's a mascot. Sort of,'
said Benji.

'He is **NOT**!' said Lexi, stomping her foot. 'My dad is a professional actor slash model.'

'Slash ball,' said CJ.

Then the music started: 'Wrecking Ball' by Miley Cyrus. It was a **FLASH MOB!** The Dancing Dads – a dance troupe made up of some fathers from school – appeared from all sides. They threw off their jackets and revealed sparkly gold tops. They all lined up behind Lexi's dad in the ball. They were bopping along, doing strange moves with their necks and pelvic work that seemed most unnatural. Plus, whenever the song's lyrics said 'wrecking ball' they all had to pretend Lexi's dad was knocking them over. Like a trust exercise, the dads at the back had to catch everyone. They were having a **BLAST**. All grinning ear to ear. If only the crowd were enjoying it as much as they were.

Lexi wasn't filming. She just stared.

'This is what you *should* get on camera.' CJ giggled as he watched his dad's belly pop in and out of his top. 'Might help them see sense!'

'For once, I'm glad my dad is always at work,' said Charlotte.

Benji grinned enthusiastically. He was loving it, copying all their moves.

Then, just like that, the music stopped and The Dancing Dads put their jackets back on and merged into the crowd.

All except Mr Li.

'Can we never speak of this again?' asked Lexi. Then she weaved through the crowd, over to her dad. He ducked out of his costume for a drink.

CJ took the opportunity to run and dive inside the big ball. He began rolling towards the turnstiles, KNOCKING PEOPLE OVER like tenpins as he went. He jumped out of the ball at the gate. 'Come on guys, now we can beat the queue!'

With Mrs Alessi trailing behind them, the kids took their seats in the North End. **NOTHING** compared to the atmosphere here. Although, Benji was starting to regret wearing his Sydney FC scarf.

As the teams took to the pitch the chants began, *Melbourne Boys Are Still Number One!*

'Come on, Bobô,' whispered Benji to himself. 'Remind everyone why Melbourne Victory are much more like Number Two!'

'Hey!' said CJ.

'Classic,' sniggered Benji.

Lexi filmed the roaring crowd with her iPad. Next to her, Charlotte took her knitting out, working on some mittens for baby Sofia as she settled in to watch the game.

The ref blew the whistle and Leroy George took the kick-off. He nudged it to the right wing. Straight to KOSTA BARBAROUSES! Within seconds, Kosta was closing in on the penalty box.

Charlotte dropped her knitting. Benji dropped his scarf. Lexi dropped her iPad. And CJ DROPPED HIS GUTS. (He'd been holding one in for ages.)

'See that? Kosta's super speedy!' said CJ. 'And it's like he has a sixth sense for booting goals. Pure instinct!'

'You know Kosta's originally from New Zealand like me, right,' said Lexi with a proud hair flick.

'Yeah, right. Sure he is,' said CJ.

'CJ, he's like pavlova, Russell Crowe and Phar Lap!' said Charlotte.

'Yeah, I know,' said CJ. 'One hundred per cent Aussie.'

Charlotte shook her head.

On the field, Barbarouses flicked the ball to Besart Berisha, who outmanoeuvred his opponent, then crossed the ball back to Barbarouses. Without wasting a moment, Kosta THUMPED the ball low and hard into the corner of the goal.

GOOOOOOAL!

The crowd went wild. CJ went even wilder.

Just like Barbarouses, CJ had always run on instinct too. Maybe that's how he'd find his boots. INSTINCT. Go with his gut. And he needed to do it in time for the big match on Saturday.

CHAPTER TEN

INSTINCT STINKS

CJ did not find his boots in time for the big match on Saturday.

And he was starting to think that instinct **STINKS**.

When CJ and Benji arrived at school for the game, the place was swarming with people prepping for the fete, so the boys didn't exactly hurry up to the pitch. This was partly because both of them were feeling nervous about the game, and partly because Miss Harmon was making DELICIOUS TOFFEE APPLES to sell at her stall and the boys were hoping she might offer them a taste. After all, the best thing about toffee apples is that you can tell your parents – without a word of a lie – that you ate some fruit!

'You're meant to be on the pitch,' said Charlotte, arriving behind them carrying a huge container of biscotti. CJ tried to sneak a sample but Charlotte KICKED HIM IN THE SHINS.

'Careful. I'm the star striker.'

'I sure hope so. We all need to step up today. Just gotta focus,' said Charlotte, then she turned to Benji. 'All of us.'

Benji pulled the peak of his cap further down over his eyes.

As CJ, Benji and Charlotte hit the football pitch, it was clear that this was no ordinary match. There were people everywhere; milling about, enjoying homemade treats, carrying balloons in Jindaberg's green and gold school colours and gossiping over coffee. By the time the other Jets arrived for the warm-up, Charlotte had to ask a bunch of ladies to give them some space.

As Charlotte performed her coin toss duties, CJ stared at his feet, willing them to do the right thing. He'd borrowed an old pair of Charlotte's boots that didn't look magical in the slightest. In fact they looked downright dull. But if they let him score, he didn't care if they looked like the Queen's fluffy royal slippers.

On the sidelines, Highpants was in deep discussion with Principal Swift. With big hand gestures and very unnatural smiles, he seemed to be assuring her that the Jets would put on an impressive show for the crowd. Baldock was behind them, shaking his head at Highpants. All the while, Garlic was PEEING on Highpants' big bag of toffee apples. TRAGEDY!

Further on, CJ noticed The Dancing Dads in the crowd. They were performing later at the fete. Hopefully MUCH later. CJ's dad gave his son a meaningful thumbs up. CJ gave a thumbs up back. Sometimes, CJ got the feeling his dad didn't know what to say to him. But a lot can be said with a good solid THUMBS UP!

Charlotte gathered the team for a final pep talk. 'Jets, I know I've pushed you hard this week, but if we want to improve we need to get *serious*.'

The Jets listened, but they were fidgety. CJ suspected Charlotte was hoping for some nods or sounds of agreement.

There weren't any, so CJ spoke up. 'I'm going to give it a crack. I hope you all do too, okay? Put 'em in!'

The Jets took a moment to react.

'I said put 'em in!'

They all reached their hands in and yelled, 'Goooooo Jets!'

CJ couldn't ignore the fact the Jets weren't responding all that well to their co-captains. As he jogged to his position he questioned Benji and Lexi, 'What's the story, guys?'

'Apart from the fact Charlotte is *Little Miss Serious*?' replied Benji.

'Or that you keep randomly treating us like we're the enemy?' said Lexi.

CJ laughed awkwardly. 'Oh *that* . . . I'm sure we'll all come together once the game gets underway.' At least, he *hoped* so.

The Rowthorn Redbacks took the kick-off. A short kid with lightning bolts shaved into his hair passed back to a determined freckly girl.

'I'll take her on!' yelled CJ. But Antonio, Fahad and Saanvi ignored him. They ran for her themselves, but she got past each of them with her fancy footwork.

Freckles sent the ball out wide to a chunky Redback wingman. CJ dropped back. The Redbacks were fast. REAL FAST.

'Need you in defence, May,' instructed CJ.

But May IGNORED him.

'Come on, guys,' muttered CJ. 'Teamwork!'

The chunky kid booted the football into space. Freckles ran to it. She had it at her feet, sailing towards the Paulveriser in goals.

'Lexi!' cried CJ. 'Hold your zone, don't get drawn in!'

But Lexi ran at Freckles.

'No!'

Freckles got around Lexi and was closing in.

CJ was on the clubrooms' wing. He heard Highpants singing from the boundary. Something with lyrics that sounded like 'Stop, in the name of love!'

The Paulveriser wore his crooked grin and bolted towards Freckles. He was like a bull, but less well-mannered.

Freckles had to take her shot before it was too late.

THUMP! SMACK!

The ball **BOUNCED** off the Paulveriser's big belly. Benji was able to mop it up.

'Think, Benji! Focus!' encouraged Charlotte.

Benji screwed up his face, trying to take the advice on board. But all that thinking and focusing wasn't working. Freckles used Benji's moment of indecision to steal the ball. She nudged it to the very corner of the goals, Kosta-style. The Paulveriser dived, but the Redbacks scored. GOAL!

The crowd clapped politely. The Redbacks jumped around hugging each other. Freckles mimed spiders with her fingers for her goal celebration.

'Chin up, Benji,' said CJ. After all, it was the WHOLE team's fault. Specifically, CJ and Charlotte had KILLED the vibe. CJ was starting to wonder more and more if he was wrong to have suspected his teammates of stealing his boots.

At the Jets' kick-off, Charlotte began shouting out their set plays. 'Peekaboo! Stinky nappy! Coochie-coochie-coo!'

The Redbacks exchanged quizzical looks. CJ was starting to wish Charlotte didn't name all her set plays after baby Sofia. He also didn't remember what most of them were meant to mean. She settled on DUMMY SPIT.

Charlotte sent the ball to a confused CJ. One thing he knew for sure was where the goals were. He tapped the ball forward and sped through two Redback defenders.

CJ must've been just a BLUR to the crowd. Within seconds he was directly in front of the goals. He wound up his leg. Then he booted the football with EVERY OUNCE OF STRENGTH in his body.

The crowd gasped at the sound of his boot SMACKING into the ball.

The football TORPEDOED towards its target.

'This is it! This is it!' exclaimed Charlotte.

But then CJ noticed the ball was curving upwards. He must've scooped it – got his foot underneath the ball too much.

It sailed **STRAIGHT OVER THE TOP** of the crossbar.

CJ fell to his knees. Charlotte came over. 'There'll be another chance.'

'Even if there is, I know I'll stuff it up,' wailed CJ. 'Unless I get my magic boots back.'

'Face it, CJ. That may never happen.'

'Don't be so sure. I've come up with a foolproof plan for half-time.'

'Huh?'

'I've laid a trap that the culprit won't be able to resist,' said CJ, grinning. 'If everything goes to plan, I'll have my magic boots back before the end of the game. And then we might just stand a chance!'

FOOTBALL FUN FACTS - Great Goal Scoring

⚽ One of the fastest goals ever scored was in 2.8 seconds by Ricardo Oliveira for Rio Negro in December 1998.

⚽ Archie Thompson scored a record five goals in Melbourne Victory's 2007 Hyundai A-League Grand Final win over Adelaide United.

⚽ Besart Berisha, holds the record for the quickest hat-trick - 5 mins 27 secs playing for Brisbane Roar in 2011. Now that's fast!

Facts checked and double-checked by Charlotte Alessi.

CHAPTER ELEVEN

FOOLPROOF OR FOOLISH?

'You should be concentrating on the game, not another one of your crazy ideas,' said Charlotte, as she jogged back into position alongside CJ.

'It's not as crazy as usual!' said CJ. 'Any minute now it'll be half-time and I might just uncover the truth!'

The Redback goalie kicked the ball back into play. It crossed halfway and a tall Redback got to it first. She ZOOMED closer to goals, sidestepping Saanvi, but she'd have to beat Benji for a clear shot.

Someone yelled out Benji's name from the crowd. He gave a little wave.

'Focus, Benji!' shouted Charlotte.

Benji's smile faded. He stared at the super tall Redback's feet, but she faked a pass and Benji took a step to block it. This was all the Redback needed to steal a metre closer to goal and go for a shot.

'Just relax,' cried CJ. 'You've got this, man!'

Benji must have heard CJ because his expression changed. His grin was back, and so were his mascot moves. Wrong footed, he used his momentum to do a handstand, then KICKED HIS LEGS up into the air just as the tall

Redback booted the ball. The ball hit Benji's foot and bounced back into the Redback, then out of bounds near the clubrooms.

'Hmmm,' said Charlotte, raising an eyebrow.

'Deserves a bit more than a *hmmm*,' said CJ. 'Go Benji!'

Benji grinned as he flipped himself upright, then started weaving through the crowd to retrieve the ball.

But then the whistle blew. Half-time. The crowd started spilling onto the pitch. MiniRoos kids kicked their balls around.

'Right, I'm staying out here for most of the break, till the very last minute,' said CJ, planting his feet firmly on the ground. 'Waiting for the thief to take the bait. Trust me, it's totally *foolish*!'

'I think you mean, fool*proof*. But what are you talking about?' asked Charlotte, annoyed that there was already a group of people in between the Jets and the clubrooms.

'Well, I've decorated my op shop boots to make them super colourful, just like my other two pairs that went missing. And I've left them right in the middle of the clubrooms. They're just *asking* to be stolen.'

'And you think someone will, what? Sneak them into their bag?'

'Yep. Might be happening right now!' said CJ with a glint in his eye.

Lexi's dad, Mr Li, arrived beside them. 'Lexi said you were after this?'

He handed CJ the Grade Five iPad.

'Thanks,' said CJ, as Mr Li returned to the other Dancing Dads in the crowd. 'You were great as the ball, by the way!'

CJ zoomed in super close on the Jindaberg map on the iPad screen. There was a blue dot flashing over the clubrooms. The title on the screen read: FIND MY PHONE.

'Whoa, I think I just worked out what you've done,' said Charlotte. 'You placed your dad's iPhone in a pair of boots you knew would be stolen?!'

'That way, if the thief is *not* a Jets' player, I'll still be able to track down whoever it is!'

'Don't mean to alarm you, but isn't that dot moving right now?' asked Charlotte.

The dot was going from one side of the clubrooms to the other.

CJ's eyes lit up. 'Gotcha!'

CJ dodged through a family eating Honey Joys and burst through the clubrooms doorway. He was the only one in the room. For the briefest moment, movement near the windows above the lockers distracted him, but his focus remained on the bench where he'd left his boots.

It was empty. The thief had **DEFINITELY** taken his boots.

A creak came from the windows. CJ got up on the bench to investigate, but all he saw was the window swing shut.

Did the thief just escape through the window?

CJ jumped a little higher to glimpse the scene outside.

There were people everywhere. There was no telling who had just left the building. But that was okay. After all, that's why he had the iPad.

The rest of the Jets entered the clubrooms, exhausted and flat. Everyone started grabbing drinks, but CJ bounded over to Charlotte.

'The boots were stolen!' exclaimed CJ with a grin. 'Look, the thief is still on school grounds. Maybe they're headed to their stash of stolen boots.'

CJ ran out of the clubrooms with the iPad in his hands.

'You'd better be back in five minutes for the second half,' called Charlotte.

Outside, the pitch was swarming with people. It was like the crowd at AAMI Park during a Melbourne Derby. CJ zoomed in on the iPad, desperate to work out where his boots were being taken. The dot seemed to be leaving the school via the main gates . . .

CJ peered down in that direction but had to shield his eyes. Glitter reflected in the sun. His op shop boots. They were leaving the school gates!

CJ ran.

He **BUMPED** into people. He **TRIPPED** over. He **SCRAMBLED** through the crowd any way he could.

'Sorry! Sorry! Super sorry! Whoopsie!'

At the school gates he saw the shape of what was probably a kid turning the corner down the street. The kid's position corresponded to the blue dot. Then a battery warning popped up on the screen, but there was no time to worry about that.

CJ was now sprinting as fast as he could, following the kid's path. He had to catch the thief and force him or her to return the magic boots before half-time was over. This was going to be TIGHT!

As CJ swept past the café, the owner shouted out, 'Stay away from my awnings, kid!'

'No promises!' cried CJ, his mind focused on running.

He turned the corner.

There was no sign of the thief.

CJ glanced up and down the street. Where had they gone? He checked the iPad again. The screen was black. BATTERY DEAD.

THINK, CJ! THINK!

He tried to put all the clues together, but his brain just seemed to bounce around in his skull. The thief could be anywhere by now. If they had the athletic skills to escape via the clubrooms' window, who knew where they'd managed to escape to.

Hang on. If the thief was a Jindaberg student, there was **ONLY ONE KID** in the whole school who had the moves to jump up and out the window like that. Someone nimble and small. *Could it be?*

The thought hit him like a **PUNCH IN THE GUTS.**

Suddenly, CJ knew where to go. He stopped at the strip of shops.

CJ was about to confront the boot thief.

CHAPTER TWELVE

GOOD GRIEF!
IT'S THE BOOT THIEF

CJ paused. He knew he had no time to waste, but did he **REALLY** want to do this? Did he **REALLY** want to reveal the culprit? Knowing it would change things. Perhaps **FOREVER**.

Yes.

Not only did the thief have his magic boots, he also had his mum's boots too. CJ couldn't let that go.

CJ was certain that the thief was . . . BENJI NGUYEN!

That's right. CJ's BEST MATE had stolen his magic boots.

Sure. It didn't make a lot of sense, but Benji was the one kid in school who could've escaped the clubrooms through that tiny window. Plus the iPad had led CJ in this direction, straight to the Nguyen family newsagency.

CJ took a deep breath and began to step inside the newsagency to confront his friend . . . or, FORMER friend.

But then he heard rustling. It was grass or trees or something, coming from the overgrown section between the Nguyen newsagency and the next shop.

Benji fell from the gap, his bum thudding onto the footpath. He shook himself, then noticed CJ. 'Dude! Am I glad to see you!'

'You sure about that?' said CJ, searching Benji's face for signs of guilt. 'Why would you *want* to be caught red-handed?'

'Huh?'

'Stealing my boots! My **MAGIC** boots.' CJ took a step closer, leaning over Benji. 'Why, Benji? You're meant to be my best mate!'

'I *am* your best mate.'

'No. You're the boot thief,' said CJ, through gritted teeth. He was too fired up to listen to the tiny thought that was nagging away at him far off in the distance. *This doesn't add up.*

'No, CJ. I'm not the boot thief . . . I'm *chasing* the boot thief,' said Benji. 'Who do you think just pushed me out of the bushes?'

CJ's face went from all screwed up and angry to wide-eyed and open-mouthed as the truth dawned on him. 'It was *Lenny*.'

Lenny stepped out of the bushes. 'Secret's out,' laughed Lenny, holding all three pairs of CJ's missing boots tied up together by their laces.

CJ's stomach swirled with a mixture of guilt, anger and even a little fear, as he helped Benji back onto his feet.

'B-b-but, why?' asked CJ. 'We used to be teammates.'

'*Used* to be,' snorted Lenny. He stepped closer to the boys. Benji backed up half a step, but CJ stood his ground. Fists clenched.

'Jeez, am I glad those days are over. I'm a Hammerhead all the way now,' said Lenny, swinging the boots in the air as he slowly paraded around the footpath. He stopped in front of CJ, holding the boots just out of reach and gave the smuggest grin CJ had ever seen. 'Remember round one?'

How could CJ forget? He and Charlotte had combined for the winning goal and it had been **DISALLOWED.**

'Well, let me jog your memory, just in case. When I left the visitors' clubrooms with the other Hammerheads, we decided to snoop around *your* clubrooms, seeing as you'd all left. Didn't find any secrets on the whiteboard though. But what I did see was these stupid sparkly gold boots. And I grabbed –!'

'I love a good prank as you know, Lenny,' interrupted Benji, glancing at his watch. 'Very funny, I guess! But are you going to give CJ's boots back now? The second half is about to start.'

'I know. I was there watching,' said Lenny. 'Although you knew that, didn't you, Benji-boy, cos you spotted me in the clubrooms swiping these beauties.'

'Even went out the window to try to block your way after you shrugged me off,' said Benji. 'Didn't work.'

'Was the Paulveriser in on this too?' asked CJ.

'Ha! Think I'd risk him opening his big fat mouth? Yeah right,' said Lenny, and with a laugh he held out all the boots in one hand, directly over the storm water drain. 'But when Pauly mentioned how badly you were kicking, I took it upon myself to keep messing with you. Stashed away quite a collection of your boots in my secret hiding spot back there.'

CJ's eyes flicked from the boots to the storm water drain and then back up to the boots. If Lenny let the boots go, all three pairs would be lost down the open drain. Forever. Lenny knew it. CJ and Benji knew it. But no-one put it into words.

Lenny grinned. 'If the Hammerheads meet the Jets in the finals, CJ, I won't have you spoiling all our fun.'

CJ tried to sneak a few centimetres closer to the boots. His brain kept repeating, GRAB THEM, GRAB THEM! But he wasn't quite close enough.

'Oh, I *so* hope we do meet in the finals, Lenny,' said CJ, inching even closer.

Lenny laughed. 'I'll bet you do.'

CJ was just about close enough now. Any second.

'And I can't wait,' said Lenny. 'Cos you'll be going . . . DOWN!'

Lenny let go of the boots. They fell. CJ lunged for them, just out of reach. His fingers swiped through the air. He saw the storm drain, water rushing furiously below, and the boots were heading for the opening.

'NOOOOOO!'

Then there was a blur of brown.

'Huh?'

It was GARLIC. He'd leapt from the footpath and GRABBED THE BOOTS in his mouth. Then he dropped them at CJ's feet.

'Nice one, Garlic!' exclaimed CJ.

'Pfft. Always been a mangy old mutt,' said Lenny, turning away. 'I'm outta here.'

'See you in the finals!' cried CJ, then he gave Garlic an enthusiastic pat. 'You really *are* a wonderdog!'

WOOF!

'Even if you did follow the scent of my boots to take us on a wild goose chase to the post box and the tip,' said CJ.

'Um, CJ. Did Garlic lead you to the post box? You realise that's right outside the *donut shop*.'

'So?'

'And the tip too, did you say? Isn't that opposite the *quarry*? They're both regular hangouts for Lenny and the Paulveriser! They must've swung by both places and Lenny probably had the boots with him the whole time!'

'Aw yeah,' said CJ. Maybe Garlic had been on the right track after all.

Benji picked up the boots. 'We better get our butts moving. Choose some boots and let's get back.'

Benji had all three pairs dangling in the air. CJ reached out.

'Did I hear you say one of these pairs is *magic*?' asked Benji, trying to keep a straight face.

CJ pointed to the pair in Benji's left hand. 'They help me kick straight.'

Benji held them out for him.

Just as he was about to grab his magic boots, CJ's mind took him back to the last time he'd seen his mum. It was in the hospital room, nearly a year ago now. CJ didn't like to think of that moment very often. His mum hadn't looked like herself. She was super thin. Pale. Tired.

CJ hadn't known what to say on that day. His mum didn't have the strength to talk anymore anyway. So he just reached out and slipped his hand under hers. Her fingers were bony. He could feel his eyes getting hot. He was sweating. But then he felt his mum squeeze his hand. Twice.

I'm thinking of you.

CJ looked at the tangled collection of boots dangling from Benji's hand. He knew exactly which pair he was going to wear. Without a second thought, he took his mum's boots.

'You sure those are the ones you want, dude? I thought the other pair helped you kick goals.'

Benji was right. CJ's magic boots had always been his secret weapon. He'd kicked his first ever goal in them, plus heaps more after that. Every time he'd scored, he'd been wearing his magic Troisi boots. But that was just a silly superstition.

CJ wanted his mum's boots. No question. When it came down to it, they were the ones he missed the most. He smiled at the thought that football ran in his family! And he was 100 per cent sure that his mum's boots were the ones he wanted to wear.

Even if it *was* a MASSIVE risk . . .

FOOTBALL FUN FACTS - Football Families

⚽ Former Socceroo Jason Davidson's father Alan was also a Socceroo. Not bad genes! Same position too: left back.

⚽ Westfield Matildas star Emily van Egmond is the daughter of Gary van Egmond, who played 15 times for the Socceroos, including at the Seoul Olympics.

⚽ The Petratos family are the first in Aussie football history to have four siblings and their father all appear in national competitions. Angelo played in the NPL, paving the way for his children, Dimitri, Kosta, Panagiota and Makis.

Facts checked and double-checked by Charlotte Alessi.

CHAPTER THIRTEEN

BOOTED!

By the time CJ and Benji weaved through the fete crowd and returned to the school football pitch, the second half of the game was well underway. The scoreboard read 1–1. At least the Jets were BACK IN IT!

'Who scored?' CJ asked Principal Swift.

'Lexi, as a matter of fact. Should make quite a popular clip for her YouTube channel,' said Principal Swift, as her big eyes swept down onto CJ's boots. 'And maybe now you'll be next, Mr Jackson.'

As usual, CJ wondered just how much Principal Swift knew about everything that had been going on, but before he could ask, Baldock started grunting at Highpants. He seemed to be suggesting that Highpants sub CJ and Benji back onto the pitch as soon as possible. And no-one disagreed with Baldock.

The boys ran on. CJ headed straight to Charlotte to help fill a gap in the midfield as the Redbacks passed among themselves, setting up to push forward. 'CJ, where the heck have *you* been? I had to do the big half-time speech without my co-captain!'

'Well, we scored. Your speech must've worked! What did you say to them?'

'Have fun.'

'*You* said "have fun"? Are you feeling okay?'

CJ and Charlotte watched the football sail out of bounds; a Redback kick had bounced off Saanvi. CJ headed down field, Charlotte ran nearby.

'The thing is, late in the first half, Benji stopped that attack on goal with one of his silly mascot moves.'

'Yep. Bit *out there*, but it worked.'

'Basically, the grin on Benji's face reminded me of the expressions The Dancing Dads had at AAMI Park, and they were dancing pretty good . . . for them. So I thought I'd try, y'know, just having fun. Anyway, whatever happens I'm going to thank Benji for the inspiration straight after the match.'

CJ nodded, impressed. 'Best idea you've had all season. The Dads also seemed to fully trust each other, didn't they?'

'Yep. Especially with their *trust* falls.'

CJ breathed in. Then he ran to the centre of the pitch and called out to his teammates. 'Jets! I know I've weirded out on you this week!'

Saanvi nodded at CJ, Antonio listened intently, and all the other Jets paused to hear what CJ had to say.

'I just want to say that I'm sorry,' said CJ, as he looked at each of them. 'But from now on, we're in this *together*!'

There was no time to ensure all was forgiven because the Redbacks threw the ball in. A smaller kid with braces started dribbling towards Charlotte. Then something weird happened: Charlotte winked at CJ. She was ENJOYING HERSELF for the first time in a while.

She ran at the kid with braces, who tried to fool her with some footwork, but Charlotte just grinned at his attempts. Then she thrust her foot at the ball, nudging it just out of his reach. She got her other foot to it and dished it off sideways to Antonio.

'Here comes the aeroplane!' yelled Charlotte. Even though this set play was also inspired by baby Sofia, it wasn't a tactic they'd ever used in a game before, only when they were mucking around at practice.

Charlotte held her arms out like a PLANE and zipped towards goal. CJ did the same thing, he even made jet engine noises. He glimpsed Principal Swift in the crowd, laughing. Highpants was scratching his bald head. Baldock was nodding ever so slightly.

Fahad sent a through ball to Charlotte. It was perfect. She and CJ jetted their way towards goal. By now the crowd were copying

the Jets' sound effects. Everyone had their arms out, pretending to be ZOOMING through the air. It seemed like the whole school fete was watching the game now.

The Redback goalie wasn't just going to wait for CJ and Charlotte to arrive. He stormed towards Charlotte. When he was almost on her, Charlotte glanced over at CJ, one eyebrow raised. CJ nodded.

GIVE IT TO ME!

Charlotte dished the football off to CJ. He had a clear shot at goal.

THIS IS IT!

Were his mum's boots going to be BAD LUCK? Should he have stuck with his magic boots after all? Was this going to be another embarrassing miss?

The jet sound effects filled the air. The crowd were laughing and cheering. Everyone was having a blast. After all, that's what football's all about.

CJ grinned and thought, *Why don't I stop thinking and just BOOT IT!*

SMACK!

CJ laughed. Whatever happened, this was awesome!

The ball soared. It rocketed up over the Redback goalie's head, then straight through the goalie's hands.

GOOOOOOOOOOOAL!

The crowd roared. It was deafening. CJ leaped skyward. 'Woooohooo!'

The Jets came running from all sides. They collided in the air, trading high fives, hugs and cheers. The group fell to the ground, everyone laughing. Then Garlic ran onto the pitch. He climbed to the top of the mountain of players and howled into the sky.

CJ's mum's boots had come through! Or maybe it wasn't about the boots at all. Maybe it was something else.

CJ's head had ended up shoved right up into Benji's armpit. 'Sorry I thought you were the boot thief.'

'That's cool, dude. I get it,' said Benji.

Charlotte had CJ's foot squished into her forehead. She looked miffed. 'Hey, you two. Aren't you forgetting something?'

Benji sighed. 'Here we go.'

'Relax, Benji, I'm talking about CJ's goal celebration!'

'Oh yeah!' cried Benji.

With CJ at the front, all the Jets stuck their arms out like planes again and ran to the corner flag for CJ's signature move. He threw his arms at the flag and spun right round it at full stretch, then landed on the pitch lying on his side. All the Jets copied, each stretched out like superstars in front of the crowd.

The ref blew the whistle.

GAME OVER!

Highpants clapped fiercely. Beside him, Baldock looked on with interest and Principal Swift cheered, 'Let's hear it for the Jindaberg Jets!'

The crowd roared. The Dancing Dads did an impromptu routine. It seemed like everyone was celebrating the Jets' victory!

CJ grinned from ear to ear as he gave his dad another thumbs up.

Their first win! 2–1 to the Jets.

And it felt **SO GOOD!**

Read on for an extract from the first book
in the series
The Champion Charlies: The Mix-Up

SMACK, BANG, CRASH!

The Champion Charlies.

That was the ACTUAL front-page headline
on the local newspaper. In big CAPITAL letters.
Right beside a 'free burger' coupon.

The page had been plastered onto the school clubroom's noticeboard since last year. The noticeboard was on the outside wall that faced the football pitch. By now the whole school had seen the article. Charles 'CJ' Jackson and Charlotte Alessi were posed in their Jets FC football gear for the photo. The shot was taken after their Grand Finals. CJ's team had just won their match in a nailbiting finish. Whilst Charlotte's team had thumped their opposition to claim the title in the girls' league. They were all smiles. They were CHAMPIONS! They were being peed on by a dog.

'Garlic!' laughed Benji Nguyen, as he exited the clubrooms and patted the kelpie on his way past. 'Your aim is worse than your breath! Get outta here, boy!'

Garlic jumped from the bench and ran off to find his owner, the school gardener, Baldock.

Benji had found what he was looking for in the clubrooms. A megaphone. Holding onto his signature Socceroos cap, Benji sprinted towards the playground beside the clubrooms where CJ was grinning maniacally on top of the monkey bars. CJ and Benji were best friends, both TOP OF THEIR FIELD. CJ was the Jets' leading goalscorer and Benji was the Jets' leading mascot. And also the *only* mascot. Not just for the Jets, but pretty much for the whole Under 11 boys' league.

Below CJ, Charlotte stood beneath the monkey bars with her arms firmly crossed. She ALWAYS wore her hair in a neat no-nonsense ponytail, but right now CJ thought her hair was pulled back tighter than ever.

'This is so NOT funny, CJ,' said Charlotte. 'If you end up in hospital, you won't be able to go to the big Matildas match with us on Thursday night!'

'Hospital! Yeah right,' said CJ with a snort.

Lexi Li had the school iPad out, videoing the whole scene, selfie-style. Lexi was the closest thing Charlotte, who could be pretty uptight, had to a bestie. As Lexi hit record, she flicked her fringe so that it cascaded perfectly over her big dark eyes. She was destined to become Insta-famous one day. Somehow she even made the Jindaberg Primary School uniform look good. Lexi moved from the football pitch to the playground, to the school chicken coop, unable to stand still. 'CJ, let me find some good lighting. If this goes viral I need to be looking my best, okay?'

CJ was balancing on top of the monkey bars. His scruffy blond hair battered by the wind. He'd whacked the seat of the swing under his arm and carried it up there till the chains stretched out horizontally from the swing's frame. There was a wild look in his eyes.

Even more so than usual. Like he'd just eaten a whole pack of Tim Tams.

The kids' football was stuck in the blooming cherry blossom tree. And the school lunch break had only just begun.

CRISIS!

'Stop wasting my time, CJ. I've allocated exactly twenty minutes to football, twenty minutes to writing a book report and twenty minutes to knitting my little sister a green and gold beanie for Thursday,' said Charlotte, checking her watch as she so often did. 'Clearly, the sensible, and *safer*, thing to do is just ask a teacher for help. Not do *whatever* you're planning. You dingbat!'

'I take that as a compliment!' giggled CJ. Then he lost his balance. He flung his free arm about to steady himself. As he regained his footing he only laughed louder. 'Relax! I've got this!'

'Come one! Come all!' announced Benji, as he finally worked out how to switch on the megaphone. His voice echoed down the slope from the football pitch to the rest of the school below. 'Watch CJ attempt another dangerous dare . . . will he fly like an eagle, or will he go the way of the dodo. Either way, you don't want to miss it!'

Charlotte shook her head at Benji as more and more kids ran over.

'Sorry, Charlotte, this is just too good to ignore,' laughed Benji. They may have all been in the same class but they didn't all share the same sense of humour. 'Gather round, catch CJ in action so you can say you saw him when he still had his teeth!'

'Get down, CJ!' snapped Charlotte. 'That old statue is in your path anyway. We can just throw a tennis ball at the football. That might knock it free.'

'Chill, Charlotte. I've got this sussed,' said CJ, rubbing his hands together. 'I'm going to leap onto this swing, fly through the air so high that I miss the statue of that old dude –'

Charlotte glared at CJ. 'Captain Jonas Jindaberg, who our home suburb is actually named after. Show some respect!'

'Yep, right over old J-Berg's head, then I'll bicycle kick in midair – like Wayne Rooney against Man City in 2011 – and boot that football right outta the tree. Game on! Simple!'

'You'll never clear the statue,' huffed Charlotte.

'Will so.'

'Will not,' said Charlotte, turning to Lexi. 'I kind of want you to keep filming this just to teach him a lesson, okay?'

Lexi looked away from the iPad to give Charlotte a thumbs up, then returned to pulling her best duck face.

Benji put his mascot moves to good use and cartwheeled beneath the monkey bars. 'Give me a C! Give me a J! What does it spell?'

'Nothing they're just initials,' said Charlotte.

'Oh yeah,' said Benji.

'Are they? I thought his name was French or something,' admitted Lexi, still smiling for the camera. Lexi and her father won a Daddy/Daughter beauty contest when she was just three, before the family left New Zealand. Ever since, she could bust out a cheesy grin in mere nanoseconds.

CJ glanced at the crumbly concrete statue. The dude was some sort of olden days ship captain. He was looking skyward, barking orders. CJ HATED following orders.

'Here I go!' cried CJ, as he put one foot on the seat of the swing. Then he pushed himself off. He started swinging. Fast. His hair whooshed straight. 'SEE YA, SUCKERS!'

The swing flew low. CJ shifted his weight, ready to somersault. About to try to bicycle kick the ball from the tree. He swung higher, and higher and then . . .

SMACK! BANG! CRASH!

CJ hit the statue. He squished right into it. Then hung onto it like it was his long lost teddy bear.

'Ouch!' cried Benji. 'I'll always remember that nose as it was, before it was shattered into a thousand pieces.'

The swing kept swinging without CJ. It smacked into the overhanging tree, and then pulled on the branch as it swung back down. The branch split off the tree and started hurtling towards the statue. CJ squeezed his eyes shut.

KERAAACK!

The broken end got lodged straight down the throat of the statue.

'That's got to clear the sinuses, folks!' cried Benji.

It looked like the statue was SPEWING OUT blossom. A huge explosion of colour was being hurled right out of old J-Berg's open gob.

'You know what? You were right, Charlotte,' grinned CJ, as he peeled his face free. 'I was never going to clear this statue.'

Charlotte shook her head.

'What on earth is going on up here?' cried Principal Swift, as she arrived on the pitch, glaring at CJ through her big round glasses that made her look like an owl.

The scene spoke for itself: kids gathered around CJ who was hugging a **SPEWING STATUE**. It was not a good look.

Charlotte spoke up. 'We were trying to retrieve the football, but –'

'But CJ took things too far?' asked Principal Swift, her big eyes bore into CJ's soul.

'It was a classic!' laughed Benji.

'Sorry. I was just super keen to play football,' said CJ. 'The season starts this weekend.'

'No it does *not*,' said Principal Swift, shaking her head at the state of the statue.

'What?' asked Charlotte.

'You heard. And this goes for both teams. This year, there'll be no football!' said Principal Swift, as she turned sharply and stormed back down to her office.

Despite all the pain CJ was in, it was Principal Swift's words that hurt the most.

NO FOOTBALL!

More adventures from

Coming soon in September 2018